SHORT TALES

GREEK MYTHS

PANDORA

Adapted by Gary Reed
Illustrated by Will Meugniot

GREEN LEVEL

• Familiar topics

• Frequently used words

• Repeating language patterns

BLUE LEVEL

• New ideas introduced

• Larger vocabulary

• Variety of language patterns

PINK LEVEL

• More complex ideas

• Extended vocabulary

• Expanded sentence structures

To learn more about Short Tales leveling, go to www.abdopublishing.com

Printed in the United States.

Adapted Text by Gary Reed
Illustrations by Will Meugniot
Colors by Wes Hartman
Edited by Stephanie Hedlund
Interior Layout by Kristen Fitzner Denton
Book Design and Packaging by Shannon Eric Denton

Library of Congress Cataloging-in-Publication Data
Reed, Gary, 1956-
   Pandora / adapted by Gary Reed ; illustrated by Will Meugniot.
      p. cm. -- (Short tales Greek myths)
   ISBN 978-1-60270-138-0
   1. Pandora (Greek mythology)--Juvenile literature. I. Meugniot, Will. II.
Title.
BL820.P23R44 2008
398.20938'02--dc22
                              2007036094

THE GREEK GODS

ZEUS:
Ruler of Gods
& Men

ATHENA:
Goddess of
Wisdom

HEPHAESTUS:
God of Fire
& Metalworking

HERA:
Goddess of Marriage
Queen of the Gods

HERMES:
Messenger of
the Gods

HESTIA:
Goddess of the
Hearth & Home

POSEIDON:
God of the Sea

APHRODITE:
Goddess of Love

ARES:
God of War

ARTEMIS:
Goddess of
the Hunt

APOLLO:
God of the Sun

HADES:
God of the
Underworld

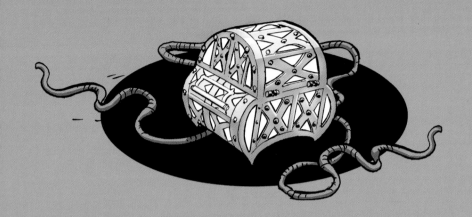

Mythical Beginning:

In the early days of Greek mythology, Zeus wanted to make new creatures that looked like the Gods. So he decided to make Man.

He had Prometheus make a man of clay and then Epimetheus was to give mankind a special gift. But Epimetheus had used up all of the gifts on the animals. So Prometheus stole fire from the gods and gave it to man.

Zeus was very upset, so he made a new creature. He made it out of clay and called it Woman. The first one was named Pandora and she received gifts from all the gods.

Pandora married Epimetheus and they had a great life of happiness. But they were given a box that they could never open. Pandora had to know what was inside.

She could not help herself. One day, she opened the box.

A long, long time ago, Zeus thought it would be good to put people on Earth.

He picked two gods, Prometheus and Epimetheus, to create humans.

Prometheus took dirt and made it into a man.

Prometheus and Epimetheus had given gifts to all the animals.

Claws, wings, shells, and many other gifts were given.

But Epimetheus had used up all of the gifts.

There was nothing left to give man.

So, Prometheus went up to the heavens.

He stole fire and gave that to man.

Zeus was very angry. He did not want man to have fire.

Zeus made a new creature out of clay.

He breathed life into it.

This creature was like man but different.

This new creature was a woman named Pandora.

Her name meant "gift of the gods."

Aphrodite gave Pandora beauty. Hermes gave her speech.

Pandora was sent to Prometheus and Epimetheus.

Epimetheus fell in love with her and they married.

But the gods had also sent another gift.

It was a box.

The box was not to be opened…ever.

Epimetheus forgot about the box.

But Pandora did not.

She wanted to know what was inside.

The box had a gold rope around it.

Pandora tried to untie it several different times.

But she could never get the knot out.

She had to know what was inside.

One day, the knot came loose.

But she had been told to never open
the box.

She thought that she would just peek.

Pandora sat in front of the box.

Epimetheus was outside and would not know if she looked inside.

But everyone said not to open it.

Then, Pandora heard voices inside the box.

They asked her to open it.

They wanted out. They were trapped inside.

"Please, let us out!" they cried.

Pandora took off the rope.

She held the lid. "Just a peek," she said to herself.

She lifted the top of the box.

As she lifted the lid, Epimetheus came in.

"No!" he yelled. "Don't open it!"

But it was too late.

The lid was opened.

Out of the box came stinging dust that covered Pandora
and Epimetheus.

Pandora shut the lid but it was too late!

The creatures were out.

The dust spread in the air and then left the house.

Pandora saw the dust become shapes.

The shapes screamed and laughed as they flew like birds.

And then, for the first time, Pandora began to feel sick.

Zeus had put all of the evil of the world into the box.

He left it with Pandora so no one would ever see it.

Now people would get sick, grow old, and feel pain.

Epimetheus yelled at Pandora for opening the box.

He had never yelled at her before.

But he had been stung so many times and he felt pain for the first time.

Pandora leaned against the box and cried.

She had never cried before.

She never had a reason to cry before.

Now the world was different.

Then Pandora heard another voice from the box.

It was a gentle voice.

It asked to be let free, like the others.

Pandora was scared to open the box again.

Epimetheus told her not to open it.

But this voice was different. It sounded so sweet.

Pandora asked is she could let the voice out.

The voice in the box said it was Hope.

It could not make the others go away, but it could help.

Pandora told Epimetheus that she had to set it free.

She opened the box again.

This time, a light breeze came out.

It was different.

It landed on her and she felt the pain go away.

Hope then went to Epimetheus.

It took his pain away also.

Then Hope left the house to chase the evil.

So, no matter how bad things got, there was always Hope.

Zeus was angry that the box had been opened.

He watched people begin to lie and steal.

Soon, they would hurt each other and start wars.

So, Zeus said it was time to start over.

He would have a flood to wash away the evil and start again.

The floods came and the water rose.

All the evil was washed away.

And all that was left were two people.

One man and one woman.

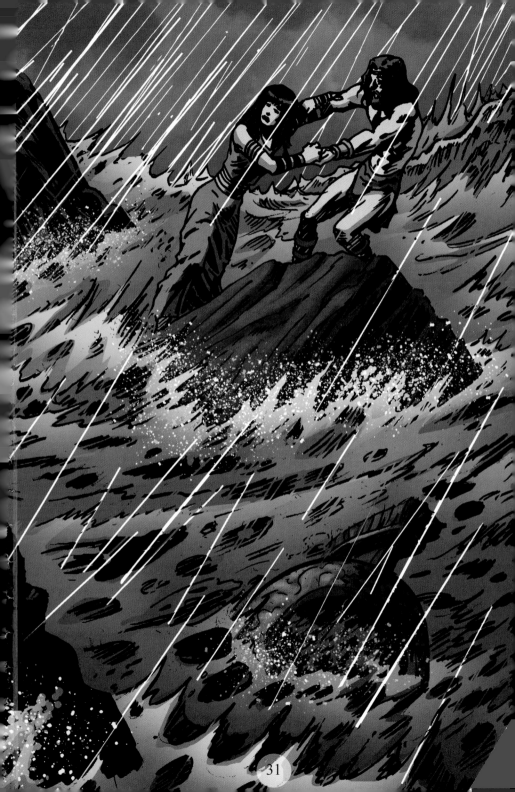

The woman was Pyrrha, the daughter of Epimetheus and Pandora.

With her husband, Deucalion, they started a new race of humans.

Although the evils were still around, so too was Hope, the last item in Pandora's Box.